GW00857378

Galaxy Voyage

Part 1

The Dragons of Doom

LDP Stead

Books by LDP Stead

Galaxy Voyage Part 1
The Dragons of Doom

Galaxy Voyage Part 2
The Sandvipers of Zaak

Galaxy Voyage Part 3
The Disc on Shard

Galaxy Voyage

Part 1

The Dragons of Doom

To Molly,

with very best wishes

L. D. P. Stead

Galaxy Voyage Part 1
The Dragons of Doom

ISBN 9781541389410

First Edition Published August 2017
Text © L. D. P. Stead 2017
Cover design © 2017 by L.D. P. Stead

www.galaxy-voyage.co.uk

On-line safety: The website address listed in this book
is correct at the time of print, but please be aware
that online content is subject to change and websites
can contain material unsuitable for children. The
publisher is not responsible for content hosted by third
parties.

For Clare, Milly and Elliot

Chapter 1

Orphan

It is a perfect day. Blue skies, birds singing, the fresh smells of spring in the air - until the attack comes.

Unprovoked, unexpected and utterly ruthless, the white terror-naught ships scream down from the skies, blasting everything in sight with hot, green lasers.

Houses explode, people scream, flames roar. The lasers cut like knives. A small boy clings to his mother. The killer robots have landed. He can hear them coming. They are close.

There is a deafening roar – a huge ship is landing right in the market square. The boy and his mother are frozen with fear, watching in horror from their hiding place. The ship lands, crushing everything beneath it.

The door of the ship slowly opens. Bright lights shine through the smoke of the fires. Then there is the sound of slow, heavy footsteps.

A tall, powerful, white robot emerges. Its armour is glowing and radiant, and a long, white cloak hangs from its enormous shoulders. The robot turns its armoured head slowly. Its face is a mask, frozen in a single expression, a slight smile fixed on its lips; its eyes completely black, unblinking they stare at the devastation all round.

"Find the boy!" commands the white robot.

"Yes! Lord Vendax!" reply the kill-bots before him, they salute and turn.

They are coming. The boy is terrified, watching the scene. His mother shakes him.

"You must run, you must hide, don't look back!" she is crying.

"No!" the boy won't let go of her.

"Go! You must go! Go now!" she shouts and pushes him away.

The kill-bots are almost on them. His mother stands and runs towards them. There is a screech of lasers and a scream.

"Mother, no!" the boy cries.

Now the kill-bots turn towards him. He runs. He runs and doesn't stop. Through the village to the woods, the branches whipping past him, thorns ripping his clothes and skin, yet still he does not stop; then he trips, and he stumbles and falls, down and down, bumping over the rocky ground into a deep pit; he is stunned, petrified in the darkness. He hides and waits, hoping for his parents' return, knowing they will not, too scared to cry.

Suddenly a cloaked figure sweeps over him, he gasps, but it is not Vendax, the arms are gentle, the words are kind, he is carried away, he is safe; but where are his parents...?

It was a dream Jack Trainer dreamed often; a nightmare from which he awoke with a terrified cry on that cold morning ten years later.

His room-mates sniggered at him.

"What's the matter, Jack, more bad dreams?" The boys ran laughing from the dormitory.

The nightmare had left Jack shaken and afraid, and this morning he wished he felt better. He had been summoned to his master's study; he

was in trouble again, and this time he
knew it would be serious.

Chapter 2

Master Stroud

"Your behaviour is outrageous! You are reckless and disobedient and you show no respect for the rules!"

Jack stood with his hands behind his back, his head down, and listened to his master.

"Here we go again!" Jack thought. "Here comes the lecture..."

"Here at Truno Abbey we offer you a simple life, a life of discipline, of patience and of self-control. We have rules to protect ourselves, to protect our secrecy and our way of life..."

Master Stroud paced the hard, wooden floor of his dark study as he spoke, his head held high; his long, brown robes hanging from his broad shoulders.

"....yet time and again you break the rules. What was it this time?" Master Stroud asked Jack.

"I was defending a friend," Jack replied through tight lips. "It was those bullies from the village – just because Lara is not human and has blue skin, they were going to hurt her... I had no choice..."

"You attacked and injured the son of a village elder!" exclaimed Master Stroud. "You broke his arm! The village leaders are very angry! You know you are forbidden from using your special fighting skills outside of the abbey."

Then Master Stroud stopped, took a long, slow breath, and looked at Jack. Jack's eye was blackened and bruised, his lip was cut.

Master Stroud smiled.

"It is sad," the master now spoke slowly, "that in a universe full of wonderful, colourful, alien races, of so many different shapes and sizes, that someone should still judge another person by the colour of their skin... – quite ridiculous, and quite awful. I do understand your actions, Jack, but there must be a consequence, there must be a punishment..."

It was at that moment that Jack's world changed forever.

"I am sorry that I have to do this, Jack..." said Master Stroud.

The flames of the candles on Master Stroud's desk flickered in the cold morning breeze. Jack straightened himself ready to hear what the punishment would be; it was worth it, to have saved Lara, and Master Stroud was always fair.

It was then that it happened -

There was a high-pitched whine of a fast approaching ship, a blinding flash of green laser bolts, and then a deafening boom as a mighty explosion burst through the room.

The stained glass windows shattered into a million tiny pieces. The books and papers on the desks and shelves cascaded in a shredded mass through the air.

Jack and Master Stroud were thrown across the room, both landing heavily on the solid, oak floor.

The breath had been knocked out of Jack's body, his ears were ringing; he looked through a stunned haze at the remains of his Master's study. Jack's body was cut and bruised from head to toe by splintered wood and broken glass, but he was alright.

"Master!..." he cried.

Jack could hear more explosions ripping through the abbey, some very close by; he could hear the screams of the monks; Truno Abbey was under attack from terror-naught ships, but why? Why would kill-bots want to attack the peaceful abbey?

Master Stroud lay on the floor. Jack could tell something was wrong. He crawled to his master. Blood covered the floor.

"Jack…" Master Stroud gasped.

Jack reached his master and kneeled by him, supporting his head in his hands, fighting back the tears. A sharp wooden shard from the windows had pierced Master Stroud's chest.

"Jack… there is so little time. It is Vendax, he is after you. They came too soon… I should have told you earlier."

"Don't try to talk, I'll get help, you'll be

fine," Jack tried to keep his voice calm, but couldn't. He knew that his master would not be fine.

Another large explosion shook the room, and dust and rocks fell from the ceiling.

"Listen, Jack, all depends on you," Master Stroud grasped Jack's shoulders as he spoke. "You have been trained here at the abbey for a special purpose. We have kept you hidden, and we have prepared you. I should have told you sooner. I have something that I must give to you..."

From inside his robes Master Stroud pulled a small, metal device, it was round, very old and was covered in strange, ornate patterns; writing perhaps, but no language that Jack recognised, and he knew many languages.

"Take this, Jack…" Master Stroud handed the device to Jack. "It is called the 'Omicron'. It is a key to unlock a powerful weapon, the only weapon which can destroy Vendax and his evil kill-bots. You must find the six crystal jewels to activate the Omicron; they are hidden across the galaxy. Use the map on the back of the Omicron to find the jewels. Now all depends on you, Jack. You must stop Vendax, or all will be lost."

Jack looked at the Omicron. He could see six holes around the edge of the device into which the jewels must fit. He turned it over and saw that the patterns on the back were indeed a map of the galaxy, but how would he read this map? How would he know where to go? Where should he start?

"But, master, I don't understand...."

"There is no time to explain, you will find the way, use your training," Master Stroud gasped.

"Jack..." The old master pulled Jack closer to him, he struggled to speak. "This is important, Jack. You must remember this. Things are not always what they seem. Be careful who you trust, and look for help in the most unexpected places. Remember, Jack, remember, things are not always what they seem..."

"But Master Stroud, I won't leave you, "Jack replied, tears burning his eyes.

"You must go! Now, before it is too late!" exclaimed Master Stroud.

Then the eyes of the old master closed, his head fell slowly backwards and he was gone.

"No!" cried Jack.

"I'll get you for this, Vendax!" Jack shouted into the dusty air. "One day I will avenge you, Master Stroud, I promise."

Then he heard the high-pitched whine of another attacking ship. Green lasers flashed.

He had no time left. He left his master and ran to the door.

Chapter 3

The Silver FOX

Jack fled from the room, flames from the explosion behind him engulfing him as he ran. His robes were on fire! He pulled them off and cast them aside; wearing only his combat training trousers and light shirt made it easier for him to move more quickly, and he had to move fast. He would not be leaving the abbey alone.

The abbey was racked by explosion after explosion. Great chunks of rock crashed to the ground, dust and smoke filled the air. Monks fled in every direction, desperately trying to find a way to escape.

Jack had been raised at the abbey by the monks after his parents died. It was the only world he knew. It had been a life of hard physical and mental training; of waking up every day before dawn, washing in freezing water, practising fighting skills, climbing the icy peaks of the mountains around the abbey, and studying information from the thousands of books in the great library.

Now Jack was glad that he knew the abbey so well. He knew its secret ways and passages. Behind a statue he pulled a hidden lever and a door opened in the wall. He jumped inside. Now he was running down a steep, circular stair case, then along a dark, damp corridor. Another explosion sent him stumbling down another set of steps, and he tumbled head long into a wooden door. It burst open and Jack fell through, rolled over and landed flat on his face on a carpeted floor.

"Jack!"

Before him stood a girl with blue skin and long, straight, dark hair.

"Lara!" Jack replied.

Lara rushed forward and helped Jack to his feet.

"I knew you would come!" Lara exclaimed, her eyes filling with tears. "What is happening?"

The friends embraced. "Thank goodness you are alright!" continued Lara, "I heard that Master Stroud's office had been destroyed. I thought you were dead."

"I'm OK," replied Jack, "but Master Stroud... he is gone."

"Why? Why would they attack here?" Lara cried, burying her head in Jack's shoulder.

"I don't know," said Jack. "Come on.

We have no time for our sorrows; we have to get out of here."

This room was their secret meeting place. It was a perfect hiding place, but today it would not keep them safe. Today they needed it for another purpose. From this room there were secret passages leading all over the abbey. Jack had counted on Lara meeting him here. He had prayed that she would have the same idea, and now they were together, it was time to escape.

"We've got to get to the ships in the hangar before they are destroyed," said Jack. Lara wiped the tears from her eyes and nodded. Sadness would come later, now it was time for action.

The two friends fled through the winding, rocky passages, down into the heart of the mountain, staggering to stay on their feet as explosions rocked the abbey above. It was here in a cave deep under the abbey that the 'FOX' ships where kept.

The FOX ships were small, agile, space flight vessels used by the monks at the abbey to get supplies from the local moon base. Now they were the only way to escape the certain death that that the kill-bots would bring.

Jack and Lara sped down dark tunnel after dark tunnel; then they climbed up through a small opening in the rock and onto a main corridor. Other abbey monks ran beside them; electrical fires sprayed sparks and flames over them as they ran. Ahead lay the FOX hangar.

They burst through the hangar door and ran for the nearest ship - 'The Silver FOX.' They ran up the ramp which closed smoothly behind them. Both jumped into the soft pilot seats of the cockpit and flicked the ignition switches. The engine roared to life.

Just then a huge explosion ripped through the hangar, and the door way from the abbey collapsed, blocking the passage way through which they had entered; no-one else would be able to escape that way. The ceiling bowed and buckled. It would not be long before the whole place collapsed on top of them.

"We have got to get out of here now!" cried Lara.

As the Silver FOX lifted off, Jack and Lara looked ahead of them and saw several other ships begin to move. 'Blue FOX', 'Red FOX', 'Green FOX' and 'Black FOX'. Some of the other monks had survived and made it to the ships too!

The engines of the little ships lit up as they swept forward towards the hangar door which was set half way up the sheer cliff on which Truno Abbey was built.

The exterior hangar door had been blasted open; fire, smoke and steam drifted across the runway, making it hard for them to see as they flew towards the opening. Red alarm lights flashed, emergency sirens wailed, and far above them, thunderous explosions continued to smash what remained of the abbey.

Blue FOX was the first ship out of the hangar, but as soon as it burst into the sunlight outside the mouth of the cave, a vicious stream of green laser bolts ripped it to pieces, and the little ship exploded in a ball of red and yellow flame.

Several terror-naughts, white kill-bot ships, had stationed themselves at the entrance of the hangar. Too large to enter, they were hovering, waiting to shoot down any FOX ships that appeared from the hangar door.

Jack and Lara both saw Blue FOX explode and gasped.

"We'll have to do this fast!" shouted Lara. "I'll fly, you get on the gun!"

Jack didn't argue. Lara was the best pilot at the abbey, and he was the best shot. He jumped up from his seat and got into position in the gun turret.

"Hold tight!" cried Lara.

Lara gave the ship full power. The Silver FOX shot out of the hangar entrance like a lightning bolt across the bright, blue sky; again the green kill-bot laser bolts blasted, but this time they missed their mark. The Silver FOX was too fast for them!

As soon as they left the hangar entrance, Jack opened fire from the Silver FOX gun turret, and red lasers streaked towards the terror-naughts.

"Take that!" shouted Jack.

The three kill-bot ships exploded in a mass of fire and twisted, falling debris.

The way was clear! The other three FOX ships, taking Lara's lead, also hit full power, and now swept safely out of the hangar entrance.

As the FOX ships swung up and turned ready to make their escape to outer space, they passed over the abbey, and a terrible sight met their eyes.

The abbey was completely smashed and ablaze. Even as they watched a final, huge explosion shattered what was left of the ancient building. Their home was utterly destroyed; all they had known was gone, forever.

However, this was no time to grieve. Above them the sky was filled with terror-naughts.

The white kill-bot ships rushed towards the FOXes in waves across the sky.

"Follow me!" Lara called into her radio.

All the FOXes turned and dived. At full speed they aimed for the ground, just pulling up at the last moment.

The terror-naughts pursued, blasting green lasers after the little FOX ships which now skimmed along the surface of the rocky planet, twisting and turning, dodging the jagged rocks which appeared before them, and narrowly evading the green rain of laser blasts which cascaded down on them from behind.

From his gun turret, Jack returned fire, his red lasers obliterating one kill-bot ship after another.

Monks in the other FOXes shot too; the sky raged with red and green laser bolts; but even as some terror-naughts exploded and smashed to the ground, more appeared to take their place and to continue the chase.

When kill-bots were ordered to destroy a target, nothing would stop them. They were fearless, ruthless and relentless.

The Black FOX was now the last of the
FOX ships, it was at full speed,
desperately trying to evade the
vicious, green lasers, but the terror-
naughts were gaining on him.

"There's too many of them!" cried the
monk from the Black FOX. Then in a
blaze of green lasers and a ball of
yellow flame, Black FOX was gone.

Now only three FOXes were left. The
Silver FOX in the lead, followed by
Green FOX and Red FOX; they turned
a sharp corner, and suddenly before
them a giant cliff barred their way;
but this was no surprise, this was what
they were heading for. In the cliff face
was a small crack, large enough for
the FOXes to fly through, but too small
for the terror-naughts. This was where
the FOXes would make their escape.

"Hold tight!" cried Lara.

The FOXes rushed into the crack in the
cliff, tilting on their sides, only just
squeezing through. Sparks flew off Red

FOX, as its hull scraped the wall of the chasm, but the pilot just managed to correct the little ship in time, and they made it through safely. The FOXes sped away in the thin gap between two mighty cliffs of solid rock.

The terror-naughts were too slow to react. Too late to turn, too large to follow the FOXes, chasing their victims at maximum speed, they were doomed. One after the other, in quick succession, the kill-bot ships slammed into the face of the massive cliff, in a giant, furious explosion of twisted metal and green flame.

"That got them!" shouted Jack.

"We're not out of this yet," replied Lara.

With a sudden jerk at the controls Lara pulled the ship upwards. Now racing up a vertical shaft in the mountain, the FOX pilots could see the sky ahead. This was it. Now was their chance to escape off the planet and into space.

Chapter 4

The Asteroid Field

The FOXes rocketed up towards the edge of the atmosphere; blue sky dropped away behind them, and they entered the darkness of space. The nearby moon hung glowing in the sky, and stars twinkled in the inky blackness.

"More terror-naughts, dead ahead!" cried Lara.

"Here we go again!" replied Jack.

In the sky ahead of them was a huge terror-naught destroyer. It was blocking their escape, and now out of the belly of the destroyer there flooded a stream of white terror-naught fighters.

"There's only one way out of here now!" shouted Lara.

"Oh no, not that way!" gulped Jack, as the Silver FOX swung round in a graceful arc.

Before them, lay an asteroid field. It was thick with asteroids of many different sizes, hanging silently in the weightlessness of space; some huge, others only tiny fragments of rock, but an impact with any one of them would spell certain destruction for the lightly-shielded FOX craft.

Only expert piloting would keep them safe; luckily Lara was the best pilot there was.

"Stick to me like glue," she called through the radio to the other FOXes, as she increased to full speed and swung the Silver FOX into the asteroid field. Red and Green FOX followed.

The terror-naughts pursued, undaunted by the asteroids, they swept after the FOXes, spouting green laser blasts from their cannons.

Immediately one of the terror-naughts misjudged his approach and exploded against an asteroid. The rest of them ignored it and accelerated even faster into the chase.

Lara spun the Silver FOX this way and that, now sweeping low over a huge asteroid, then arcing up into a clearer passage between the giant, looming rocks, twisting and turning at break-neck speed.

Jack was blasting at the asteroids to clear a way ahead, then spinning the gun turret round to take a shot past the other FOXes at the pursuing terror-naughts.

"Keep up, FOXes! This way is our only chance!" cried Lara.

Behind them the pilots of Green FOX

and Red FOX were struggling to keep up, and all the time the terror-naughts were gaining.

Then Green FOX turned too sharply, his wing clipped an asteroid, spinning the small craft into the path of the approaching kill-bot ships. Terror-naught laser beams cascaded down onto Green FOX, and in a blazing explosion he was gone.

They were not far from the end of the asteroid field now. Once out the other side they could use the space-fold engines and speed safely away.

"Just a few more seconds!" called Lara. Then they were out the other side and into clear space. The Silver FOX and Red FOX sped away from the asteroid field.

"Setting the co-ordinates for space-fold!" called out the pilot of Red Fox. His fingers desperately tapped the information for the space-fold jump into his navigation computer.

But the terror-naughts were closer behind him than he realised. Gushing out of the asteroid field at full speed, they blasted the Red FOX with hot, green, laser destruction. The Red FOX exploded, and was no more.

Now the kill-bots turned their ships after the Silver FOX. In open space the greater size and speed of the terror-naughts gave them the advantage. In moments, they were right behind Jack and Lara.

Lara swung left, then right, evading the green laser blasts, but not fast enough! They were hit! An explosion racked the little ship, smoke filled the cockpit, but still the Silver FOX survived.

Lara tried to type into the navigation computer, but couldn't complete the sequence for space-fold as well as fly the ship to avoid the terror-naught laser blasts.

"Anytime you're ready!" shouted

Jack, as he swung the gun turret to and fro blasting red laser beams at the pursuing terror-naughts.

His shots were good, and repeatedly found their mark, saving the Silver FOX from certain destruction time and again.

"I am trying!" replied Lara, as she typed with one hand onto the navi-com, at the same time swinging the little ship up and round, narrowly dodging a stream of laser blasts which had evaded Jack's defensive fire.

If they didn't fold space and jump to hyper-speed in the next few seconds, the terror-naughts would have them.

Suddenly, another ship was ahead of them. It was flying straight at the Silver FOX. Lara gasped, instinctively raising her hands in front of her face, expecting the impact and explosion which would finish them, but instead something very strange happened - The terror-naught ahead of her turned at the last moment, and out of its escape hatch a kill-bot launched itself towards them. Its metal hands clamped onto the wing of the Silver FOX, and it clung there.

The kill-bot's ship span off, out of control, and collided with the first of the pursuing terror-naughts, buying Lara precious moments to complete her flight calculations.

She took advantage of this strange turn of events. With a few, final, expert taps of her fingers, she completed the calculation sequence for space-fold.

"Hold tight!" she shouted, and punched the hyper-speed button.

The lights of the console in front of Lara appeared to twist and bend, the stars became streaking blurs across the sky, and the deep, echoing boom of the space-fold engines shook the ship. Lara and Jack were thrown back in their seats as the Silver FOX sped away into the depths of space.

They had escaped, but as they flew at hyper-speed, the Silver FOX juddered and shook. They had sustained too much damage.

Emergency lights flashed all over the console, and Lara knew they would never make it.

Chapter 5

Centurion 42

As the Silver FOX hurtled through the fold-tunnel, Jack and Lara peered through the cockpit window at the kill-bot still clinging to the wing.

"What is it doing?" asked Lara. "I've never seen one act like this."

"I don't know, but let's not wait to find out," replied Jack. Opening the weapons locker, he took out a laser crossbow, and clicked the activate button. It was his favourite weapon, powerful and deadly accurate.

"It's moving towards the damaged giro-controller!" cried Lara.

Jack looked from the window again and watched as the kill-bot slowly edged its way towards the sparking, smoking areas of the wing which had been hit by the terror-naught laser blast.

The swirling winds and currents in the fold-tunnel threatened to tear the robot free to certain destruction at any moment; yet steadily it moved until it reached the damaged circuit boards. Holding fast with one hand, it reached forward with the other, and began to bend and twist the wires.

"What's it doing? It's going to make us crash!" cried Lara.

"No! Look at the controls. It's stabilising the ship!" answered Jack.

The ship was indeed stabilising. The kill-bot had saved them. Then from the radio transmitter came a voice.

"Help me, please." It was a deep metallic, synthetic sounding voice.

"It's the kill-bot!" exclaimed Jack.

"It must have tapped into the com-system," agreed Lara.

"Please help," the kill-bot repeated its desperate plea.

Jack and Lara looked out the window. The kill-bot's face was turned towards them.

"I will not harm you. I was sent to help you. Please trust me. I cannot hold on for much longer." The kill-bot's calm, electronic voice showed no sign of panic, but Jack and Lara could see that in moments he would be destroyed.

Jack and Lara looked at each other.

A kill-bot had never behaved like this before. They were simple, ruthless, killing machines.

Then suddenly, Jack remembered the last words of his master:

"Things are not always what they seem... look for help in the most unexpected places... remember things are not always what they seem..."

Had Master Stroud known about this?

"Who sent you to help us?" asked Jack.

"Your Father," the kill-bot replied.

Jack was stunned. Lara gasped and looked round at Jack.

"My father? But he is dead. He died when I was very young. How could you know him?" demanded Jack.

Jack had always been desperate to know more about the mother and father he could barely remember. He had only been six years old when Vendax and his kill-bots had destroyed his village and killed his parents. He alone had survived; saved by Master Stroud.

Master Stroud had been like a father to Jack; but Jack had always wanted to know more about his real father and mother. Could this be the chance to know more?

"What are we going to do?" Lara asked, pulling Jack out of his thoughts.

"We can't trust a kill-bot!" exclaimed Jack. Suddenly the anger returned; anger at Vendax and at all kill-bots. They had killed his parents, destroyed his village, and now they had destroyed the abbey and his master too.

Just then, a strange noise drifted from the radio.

"Is that singing?" asked Lara.

From the radio came the kill-bot's metallic voice and it was singing! The melody was gentle and sweet, a lullaby. Jack froze, he knew it at once.

"My parents used to sing me that song

to send me to sleep!" whispered Jack. "I've not heard that song in a long time..."

Jack's eyes glazed over as he recalled his childhood room in his parent's quaint cottage, set in idyllic countryside, rolling hills, sunshine, a cool breeze, perfect, safe and happy. He imagined his parents' faces for the first time in many years. The song had brought it all back.

The kill-bot must have a connection to his parents.

"Please trust me. I am slipping. I can help you," the kill-bot spoke again.

The song had stopped, and Lara and Jack looked out at the kill-bot, which now barely clung on to the wing.

"Take us out of fold-speed. Open the emergency hatch," said Jack.

"Are you sure?" asked Lara.

"No," said Jack, "but do it anyway."

"OK," replied Lara, sounding unsure.

Both Lara and Jack knew the risk. It might be a trick, the robot might tear them and the ship to pieces as soon as it entered the air-lock; but why had it not tried to destroy them already? Why had he helped them escape the terror-naughts? Why had it repaired their ship?

Neither of them had heard a kill-bot speak so normally, let alone sing. It almost sounded human. Perhaps it could help them, and it seemed to know something about Jack's father.

Lara understood Jack's need to know more about his parents. She too was an orphan. The monks at the abbey had found her when she was a baby, tiny and alone. No-one knew who had left her; she did not know where she came from or where her race lived. She was the only one of her kind. She would probably never find her family, but if there was a chance that Jack could find out about his, she would do all she could to help.

Lara pulled the ship out of fold-speed, and brought it to a full-stop. Jack opened the air-lock, and the seven foot tall kill-bot heaved itself inside the Silver FOX.

Jack and Lara were ready. Jack armed with his crossbow and Lara with a laser spear.

"Thank you," said the kill-bot in its deep, sonorous voice. "My name is 'Centurion 42'; I am very pleased to make your acquaintance, Jack Trainer."

Chapter 6

The Omicron

"I know that you don't trust me, and I don't blame you, Jack." Centurion 42 continued in his low voice, "but you must believe me that I will cause you no harm and that I have been sent to help you. Your father - John Trainer, reprogrammed me at the deepest level. I don't know how, and I cannot remember when, but my circuits have been completely re-organised. It is now impossible for me to hurt any life form, and my primary mission is to protect you, and to help you."

Jack's head was whirling. Too much had happened today, he didn't know where to begin; he had so many questions rushing through his mind. How had his father known this robot could help him?

Lara put a hand on Jack's arm and turned to Centurion 42.

"Prove that you will not harm us," demanded Lara.

"I cannot," replied Centurion 42. "Trust must come in time; but I can place my life in your hands, as a gesture of good faith."

The robot opened a control panel in his chest and pointed to a small circuit board.

"Take it, deactivate me. Decide what to do with me. If you decide to trust me, I will help you and protect you. You have my word. If you decide that you cannot trust me, I understand. Do not re-activate me. I will not wake up, and I will never know what happened. I place my life in your hands."

Lara reached forward with a quick movement and pulled out the chip.

The giant kill-bot froze; the hum of his internal electronics and servo-motors suddenly fell silent. Centurion 42 was motionless, powerless - asleep.

Jack and Lara looked at one another. A kill-bot would never normally allow itself to be treated so. It would always fight to protect itself. Perhaps they could trust Centurion 42?

They would decide later, for now they needed to think. Where should they go? What should they do? Jack knew exactly where to look for answers - the Omicron.

Jack took out the device and showed it to Lara.

"What is it?" said Lara running her fingers over the strange markings on its metallic surface.

"Master Stroud gave it to me just

before he died," replied Jack.
"He told me that it is called the
'Omicron'; it is a key to unlock a
powerful weapon. I have to find the
six crystal jewels which fit in these
holes; then it will activate a secret
weapon which can destroy Vendax
and his armies."

"How do you know where to find the
jewels?" asked Lara.

"There was a map," said Jack, turning
the Omicron over. Lara and Jack
peered at the markings.

"It looks old, but the engraving on the
back is more recent – a map of the
galaxy," said Lara turning to the navi-
com and bringing up a galaxy map
on the screen.

"Look, this must be the route we need
to take," said Jack.

He ran his finger along a dotted line
that spiralled around the map, it
passed through six star-systems. Six

star-systems, six jewels to find. It made sense.

"The first star-system is here," continued Jack, pointing to where the dotted line began. "What are these numbers – '4/7'? What can that mean?"

"That star-system has seven planets," said Lara.

"So it's the fourth planet out of the seven planets in that star-system?" suggested Jack.

"Yes, it could be," replied Lara, although she sounded uncertain, "but how in the stars are we going to find a single jewel on a whole planet? We don't even know for sure that '4/7' means the fourth planet. It is a big galaxy out there, Jack. Are you sure that this is all a good idea?"

A look of determination came over Jack's face.

"I have to try, Lara," said Jack. "I owe it to Master Stroud, to all the monks at Truno Abbey who cared for me and lost their lives. I owe it to my mother and father and to all the people of my village who died when Vendax attacked. They died, but I lived. I will not forget them, I will not forget what happened and I will honour their memory by doing all I can to solve the riddle of the Omicron, to find the jewels which activate it, and to use the weapon to destroy Vendax. I don't know if this planet 4/7 is the right place to start; but I am going to try."

Jack and Lara stopped. They looked at one another. The Silver FOX hung silently in space. Suddenly, it hit them. They had escaped, but everyone and everything they had known was destroyed.

For a moment they held each other, tears stung Jack's eyes and a lump closed his throat, but he swallowed it away. There were too many tears to cry and too little time for sorrow.

They may have escaped to fold-speed, but they could not just hang around in deep space, it would be too easy for the kill-bots to detect them.

"Well, if you are going to do this, then I am coming with you!" smiled Lara, and hugged Jack.

Jack blinked away the tears and smiled. "How can we fail? You, me and the Silver FOX! We'll be unstoppable!" he said.

"And don't forget," Lara continued, "you also have your very own house trained kill-bot too!" She pointed to the motionless Centurion 42.

Jack laughed and shook his head. He had forgotten for a moment that they still had the mystery of the kill-bot to unravel.

"Of course, how could I forget?" Jack said. "What a team!"

Lara smiled. Even in the face of total disaster, Jack's good humoured nature shone through.

"Now, what is this planet 4/7? What is the fourth planet of that star-system?" asked Jack, as they both slid into the pilot seats and strapped themselves in ready for space-fold.

Lara was already tapping swiftly into the navi-com.

"You'll love this," she grimaced. "The planet is called 'Doom'!"

"Oh good! What a great start!" groaned Jack.

Then, with a punch of a button, Lara fired the space-fold engines, and the Silver FOX shot off towards the planet Doom.

Their voyage across the galaxy had begun.

Chapter 7

Doom

The Silver FOX pulled out of hyper-speed. The space-fold engines powered down, and the planet Doom filled the front view screen.

Jack and Lara gazed out at the planet. Neither of them had been here before. It was blue and green, with swirling, white clouds making spiral patterns over its surface.

Suddenly a clear, slow, steady bleep began to come from the Omicron. Jack took the device and showed Lara.

There was a light flashing in time with the bleep; it was shining from the centre of the planet marked 4/7.

"It looks like your idea might be right!" smiled Lara.

"Yes, and look, as I move the Omicron, these arrows light up; whichever way I turn it, the arrows point towards the planet," said Jack.

"It has a direction finder!" replied Lara. "This might be easier than we thought. Place the Omicron on the navi-computer and I'll see if I can align the signal and display the target on a map of the planet."

The steady bleep from the Omicron continued, as Lara tapped at the keys of the navi-com. A map appeared on the screen; it was the surface of the planet Doom below them.

"Now to find the source of the signal," Lara said as she continued typing.

The word 'Searching...' appeared on the screen.

"Come on," Lara mumbled to the computer.

Jack watched her at work. There was nothing she couldn't get a computer to do!

"There! Easy!" exclaimed Lara, a grin spreading wide over her face as a flashing red dot appeared on the map of Doom on the screen.

"That's amazing!" smiled Jack. "Can you get us there?"

"Already on our way!" replied Lara.

The Silver FOX descended towards the surface of the planet. Jack could see their route marked out on the map displayed by the navi-com.

Gradually they approached the spot marked with the pulsing red dot. That was where they would find the first jewel for the Omicron; this was going to work!

As they entered the clouds, their view was lost, the view-screen now just white, blasted by beads of moisture. Then suddenly, they broke out under the clouds, and before them lay the vast jungles of Doom.

As far as the eye could see, the dense, tangled trees spread into the distance; swathed in curtains of mist and teeming with life. The sunlight sparkled on a wide river which snaked its way between the trees off towards the distant horizon. On the small patches of open ground near the river, herds of wild animals moved slowly as they grazed, and birds filled the sky in large, graceful formations.

From out of the forest canopy, tall, twisted spires of orange rock spiralled upward, like gnarled fingers pointing to the sky. Some stretched hundreds of metres above the tree-tops. Flocks of large birds circled in thick concentrations about the tops of these thin, high rocks.

"Wow!" said Jack.

The view was breath-taking, and both Jack and Lara gazed in awe from the windows of the Silver FOX at the incredible spectacle before them.

"All this was underwater once," said Lara, glancing at the information being relayed by the navi-com. "The rock was worn away by a giant river, then, as the waters receded over millions of years, all that was left were these spires of rock - fascinating!"

"Lara really loves her geology - and her history!" thought Jack.

"The signal is coming from over there," continued Lara.

The map on the navi-com became more and more detailed as they homed in on the signal from the jewel. Now Jack could see that the flashing signal originated from the top of an extremely tall, rock spire, which twisted high above the forest, dwarfing all the other rocks around it.

Lara flew towards the high peak and made a long, slow circle about it to get a good look.

Near the top of the tall, orange rock was the mouth of a cave; and it was from inside the cave that the signal came.

"That's got to be it," smiled Jack, "and you said it would be hard to find!"

"Hmmm... " said Lara raising her eye brows. They both knew they would never have found it without her computer expertise.

"Look at that!" cried Jack.

The large birds flying around the tall spire of rock had suddenly stopped their effortless gliding and had flocked together in a large arrow-head formation, and although they were still some way off, they were flying directly towards the Silver FOX and were moving fast.

"Strange," said Lara, "not how birds usually behave....."

Jack's face fell. "Those aren't birds! Quick, turn the ship around!"

"Why, what are they?" asked Lara.

"Dragons!" replied Jack.

Lara pulled the ship around, but even Jack's keen eyes had spotted the danger too late.

Suddenly, the view screen was a blur of scraping talons and red scales. The mighty beasts hurled themselves at the Silver FOX. Diving aggressively at the small ship, they reached out with long claws, trying to get a hold, teeth scraping along metal, and heavy bodies impacting on the hull of the FOX, smashing into it and causing it to rock violently to one side, then the other.

Lara struggled to maintain control of the little craft. She and Jack were thrown from side to side in their chairs, as wave after wave of the dragons attacked.

Then a particularly huge beast reached out with both its hind legs and for a moment its talons managed to grasp the wings of the Silver FOX. With a great, thrusting, twisting motion, the dragon flipped the ship.

Black smoke gushed out of the wing, as the Silver FOX span over and over, falling from the sky, spiralling down, out of control, towards the jungle below.

Chapter 8

Crashed!

Lara desperately struggled with the controls, trying everything she could to stop the Silver FOX from crashing.

Yet still the little ship span round and round, plummeting to the ground. She pulled back on the controls with all her might.

"Hit the stabilisers!" she called to Jack.

Jack couldn't reach the controls for the stabilising thrusters, the G-forces of the spin were pinning his hands to the chair; but he strained with all his might and timing it just right, he managed to push the auto-stabilise button.

That did the trick; the Silver FOX
stopped spinning, but they were still
heading straight down to the ground
at break-neck speed.

Jack tapped the console again, and
the nose thrusters gave the ship just
enough lift to stop a direct vertical
impact, but they were still going to
crash!

"Hold on!" shouted Lara.

She threw all power to the forward
shields to give them as much
protection as she could, but in front of
them in the view screen the tree-tops
surged closer and closer, as the Silver
FOX streaked headlong towards the
jungle canopy.

With a sudden, crunching impact,
they hit. Tearing through the forest,
blasting leaves and branches in all
directions, the Silver FOX ripped
through the trees. Lara tilted the ship
this way and that to dodge the main
tree trunks; their only chance was to

control the crash in the thinner branches.

"I'm going to start the landing sequence!" she shouted over the whining engines.

The little craft shook, as the shields were battered by impact after impact with the tangled, jungle branches; but Lara just managed to keep the ship level, and the contact with the trees had slowed them down.

The landing cycle began, retro-thrusters fired, and finally, bursting through dense bushes into a small clearing, with the painful sound of wood and shrubbery crunching and grinding against the metal hull, they came to juddering halt.

Lara and Jack collapsed back in their chairs. They had made it - but only just, and what damage had the Silver FOX sustained? Could it fly again or were they stuck here for good?

"That was too close!" Jack said.

A short while later, Jack and Lara emerged from the Silver FOX. The jungle was hot and steamy; the air echoed with the calls of wild animals. They walked round the ship and looked at the damage.

"Well, it could be worse," said Lara.

"But it's not good," replied Jack.

Lara nodded in agreement.

The shields and Lara's fancy flying had protected the Silver FOX from much more serious damage; but it would take them a long time to repair the ship to make it space-worthy.

"I have an idea," said Jack.

He climbed back up the service-ramp into the FOX and began gathering bits and pieces of electronic equipment from the store compartment.

"What are you doing?" asked Lara.

"You'll see," smiled Jack.

She left him to it. Jack was an expert at electronics and circuits, but when he was working it was best to leave him alone!

An hour later, Lara had just finished running self-diagnostics and repairs on the main computer when Jack called to her from the cargo hold.

As she entered the hold she jumped and grabbed for her weapon. Centurion 42 stood in front of her. He was very much awake and armed with a welding tool.

"Please don't be afraid," said Centurion 42, in his deep, metallic voice. "I will not harm you."

"No," said Jack, "he won't! - watch this!"

Jack appeared from behind the giant

kill-bot and pressed a button on a small device strapped to his wrist. Immediately, Centurion 42 fell still and silent. Then Jack pressed the button again, and the robot came back to life.

"I promise I will not harm you..." Centurion 42 began, and again Jack pressed the button and the kill-bot was shut down once more, his voice slurring off into silence, his arms dropping to his sides.

"See?" smiled Jack, "you said I had my very own kill-bot, and now I do! I have total control."

Jack pressed the button once more, and Centurion 42 came back to life.

"I understand why you feel the need to do this," the Centurion said, "but I want you to know that it is a very disconcerting experience."

"Well, if you want to earn our trust, this is the way it's going to be," said Jack.

"I understand," said Centurion 42.

"Now - I have uploaded all the information you need to repair the ship," explained Jack.

"I understand," the kill-bot said again. "Do you wish me to begin?"

"I certainly do!" smiled Jack.

Lara stepped back to let the kill-bot pass.

"Impressive!" she said.

Centurion 42 was extremely efficient at repairing the ship. He was able to work at ten times the speed and with far greater accuracy than either Jack or Lara could hope to have managed.

Whilst the Centurion completed the repairs, Jack and Lara worked out the quickest route to the cave at the top of the rocky spire that they had seen before the dragons had attacked, and where they hoped to find the first Omicron jewel.

By evening, they were in good shape. The main repairs on Silver FOX were nearly complete, and they had planned a route to the cave.

Jack deactivated the kill-bot and they both tried to settle to sleep; but the eerie noises of the jungle outside kept startling them awake. They activated the shields to protect the ship and every so often they heard a fizz or a crunch as inquisitive jungle creatures tried to approach them, but were repelled by the invisible electric force field. Eventually they fell into an uneasy sleep, exhausted by the events of the day.

At first light they were ready to depart; wearing back packs with all the equipment they thought they might need, and armed - Jack with his cross-bow and Lara with her laser-spear. They needed to travel fast, they had a long way to go, and neither of them wanted to be caught out in the jungle at night time.

"What about 42?" asked Lara.

"I have programmed him to complete the repairs on the Silver FOX," said Jack. "If he deviates from the instructions it will cause him to automatically shut down. I can monitor him with this." Jack raised his arm to indicate the watch-like device strapped to his wrist.

"Let's get going!" continued Jack. He activated the Omicron; it pointed the way in which they should travel.

"See you later, 42!" said Jack.

"Good luck," said the Centurion.

Chapter 9

Claws

They made their way through the dense jungle of trees and plants of every imaginable shape and size. Waterfalls cascaded down into pools where luminous algae caused incandescent eruptions to spray from the surface of the water; giant, bright, fluorescent flowers, spectacular in their dramatic shapes and decorated with complex, intricate patterns, attracted insects of infinite variety which flew, hopped and crawled on every surface.

The sounds of animals near and far filled the moist air - the high-pitched calls of birds, croaking reptiles and the deep, echoing barks of large predators defending their territories. It was at once spectacular and terrifying.

Jack stopped to look at the Omicron by a thick, gnarled tree trunk covered in twisted vines. A sweet smell like honey filled the air, and for a moment he stopped, breathed deeply, and felt calm and peaceful.

The lights on the Omicron showed clearly the direction in which they should travel, and Jack smiled. Things were finally going their way.

Jack thought he felt something move past his leg. He quickly glanced down, but there was nothing. He smiled again, just his imagination!

Jack gazed out into the jungle, it was so beautiful, and the sounds of bird calls became a calming, relaxing melody.

The vines from the tree were slowly moving and twisting themselves lightly round his ankles; it felt soothing and gentle, this place was amazing; he loved it here.

"Wait a minute!" he thought, shaking his head. "The vines are doing what?"

He looked down and saw the vines wrapping themselves around his legs, and now they were squeezing more tightly. He tried to break himself free, but the vines just gripped even more firmly, and more were moving, taking hold of his waist and now his wrist and arms.

"Lara!" he shouted.

Suddenly the vines moved more quickly, wrapping themselves all around him and pulling him up into the branches above.

Lara ran towards the tree and looked up after Jack as he was hauled away into the thick leaves. She gasped, for there tangled in the branches, entwined with vines, were the skeletons of the carnivorous tree's previous victims. It was a giant, meat eating plant, and Jack was its next meal!

As Jack looked about him, he began to come to his senses. The smell of honey must have been an airborne narcotic, designed to attract and intoxicate the victims of the meat-eating tree.

Now Jack was completely entwined and was being drawn into the trunk of the tree, and to a slow death; his face squeezed towards the gaping mouth of a monkey skeleton. The hapless simian must have been lured to the tree and sedated with the same euphoria-inducing toxin that had overcome Jack.

Jack struggled to take it all in, his brain still confused by the intoxicating spores emanating from the tree.

In his drugged state, Jack noticed something else. He was not alone with the skeletons in the tree; another creature had been captured and was still alive. The animal had purple fur and was cat-like in appearance, with large, green eyes and long, white whiskers. It looked at Jack, clearly intelligent, but also confused and delirious from the effects of the intoxicating spores.

Lara leapt into action. She quickly climbed up a nearby tree and carefully made her way along a branch towards the vines of the tree which held Jack. She balanced using her laser-spear, and as she approached the killer vines, she activated the weapon.

With a throbbing hum, a red laser emerged from the tip of the metal rod, and with another click of a switch, a second laser point appeared from the other end to form a double-ended, laser-spear.

Lara began to swing the spear round in a circle with expert skill. It span rapidly, and in Jack's blurred vision it became a red, glowing circle whirling about her head. Holding her breath to protect herself from the narcotic spores, Lara plunged forward and sliced the vines holding Jack. Lara's strokes were absolutely precise, and Jack felt himself fall free from the trap. He slipped down the trunk of the tree and rolled away from it as fast as he could.

Immediately his head began to clear, and he shouted up to Lara.

"There's something else up there! Look, in the vines!" he called urgently, determined to free the desperate creature caught in the same snare that moments ago had hold of him.

Lara peered into the vines, unable to take a breath for fear of becoming drugged and falling into the trap herself; she lunged forward again to try and set the feline creature free.

This time the tree seemed to sense her presence, and vines began to reach out towards her. She deftly severed them with blows from her laser-spear and with a well-aimed, arcing sweep of her long, laser-tipped weapon, she cut the vines holding the cat, and it was free. It rolled down the tree trunk, reaching out with its paws to slow itself down as it fell, leaving deep, long claw marks in the trunk of the tree which had been its captor, and which would have certainly eaten it alive, had it not been for Lara.

The feline creature rolled away from the tree, ending up in a crouched position and hissed at the vines which still wriggled about the tree-trunk.

The cat-like creature looked up at Lara, and slowly it stood up on its hind legs. Its body was muscular and sleek, covered in purple fur, except for its chest which was white. As it stood up to its full height, standing on its hind legs, it now extended its arms, and to their surprise, it had not two arms, but four; so it could run cat-like on six legs, or stand upright like a person and have the use of two pairs of arms. Over its shoulder there hung a bag, and around its waist was a belt on which hung leather pouches and four holsters, each containing a laser pistol.

This was clearly not a wild animal, but an intelligent, sentient being. The creature placed a pair of his arms across his stomach, extending the other pair of paws out to the side; with an elegant flourish, and in the most chivalrous and sophisticated manner, it bowed to Lara in gratitude for her rescue.

Lara and Jack smiled, and Lara bowed back in return.

Jack and Lara introduced themselves to the creature and explained their mission. They didn't tell him everything, they were cautious about who they should trust, but they told him that they had crashed, and that they were searching for something high in the cave at the top of the spire mountain and that they could not leave without it.

The cat-like creature listened carefully and seemed to understand them completely, but was unable to speak in any language Jack and Lara could understand. He expressed himself with a range of feline noises – long, deep, growls, rolling meows and humming purrs. He also used his four strong, arms, in clear, dramatic gestures, to reinforce what he was trying to say.

He was a calm, quiet and dignified creature; his face was like a lynx, his ears formed to points and were topped with tufts of white fur; they twitched expressively as he listened. He had long whiskers, and on his chin the white fur formed a wispy, little beard. His large teeth, sharp claws and muscular physique left Lara and Jack in no doubt that he was a formidable warrior. Yet he was humble and polite. Jack and Lara took an instant liking to him.

Then the cat-creature beckoned them to follow him. They looked at each other, then followed as he led them into the jungle. It was in the direction they needed to go, and they felt obliged to see what he wanted to show them after he had listened so intently to their story.

They had not gone far when they entered a clearing, and there was a small ship. Much smaller than the Silver FOX. It must have been some kind of escape pod. Next to it was a make-shift shelter and the remains of a small camp fire.

The cat extended his four arms in a gesture of resignation.

"Have you crashed too, are you stuck here?" Lara asked.

The cat nodded sadly.

"Come with us," Jack insisted. "We

have a ship." Jack motioned the flight of a ship with his hands.

The feline creature immediately understood and nodded enthusiastically.

"Come on then!" said Jack.

"But first - the cave," added Lara.

Again the creature nodded. He touched his chest and extended his arms towards Jack and Lara, at the same time making a slow, low, growling, meow sound.

Jack and Lara felt sure that they understood him.

"You will help us?" Jack checked.

The cat nodded, baring his teeth lightly into a smile, and once again he bowed low.

It seemed that their Galaxy Voyage had a new member of the team!

"What should we call you?" Lara asked.

The cat pulled himself to his full height, and with a long, rich, complex mixture of feline sounds, he spoke his name.

The sounds lasted for more than twenty seconds, and Jack and Lara listened in stunned silence.

"Ppppprrrrrouuoooowlllrrrgrhhgggggrh hhhhlaaawwwrrrrrrrrllllllllgraa... "

Then right at the end, the sounds turned into a clear, pronounceable word:

"..pppprrrgghhrowlrrrgrrrr...claawws".

"Wait did you say....'Claws'? Can we call you 'Claws'?"Jack asked tentatively.

The cat-creature stopped.

'Claawss!' he said in a tone filled with sumptuous, feline expression.

Then his shoulders seemed to shake a
little, his mouth opened slightly, and
he began to utter little noises in his
chest which could only be laughter.

"Claawws!" he repeated, still giggling,
he extended one arm and showed
five razor-sharp, inch-long claws.

"Claws!" Jack and Lara repeated.
The creature smiled and nodded, still
giggling.

"'Claws' it is then!" said Jack.
Then he and Lara seemed to catch
the cat's infectious giggles and began
to laugh too.

After all the danger, fear and stress, it
felt good to meet such a friendly
creature, and the name suited him
just too perfectly! It felt good to laugh.

"And I am Jack," said Jack touching
his own chest, "and this is Lara,"
extending his arm towards his good
friend.

Then both Jack and Lara bowed low to the cat, just as he had done to them, and they all laughed again.

"Welcome to the team, 'Claws'!" laughed Jack.

Chapter 10

Spire Mountain

Jack, Lara and Claws made their way through the dense jungle to the foot of the enormous spire of orange rock which stretched up past the tops of the trees and then up for hundreds of metres into the blue sky of Doom.

Claws had taken a few possessions from his crashed ship, including a rope; and now the three of them stood at the base of the rock and stared up.

"It's going to be quite a climb," said Jack.

"Well, let's get started then," said Lara.

"It won't be long until it's dark."

Claws held out the rope and indicated that he would go first. The three tied themselves to the rope, and Claws led the way up the vertical rock.

Claws was an expert climber. With his six legs, his tail for balance, sharp claws for extra grip and great strength, he easily and steadily made his way up the cliff.

Jack and Lara were also excellent climbers, they had both grown up climbing in the mountains around Truno Abbey; it was second nature to them, but even for them this rock was a challenge.

Soon the three of them had passed the tops of the trees and were now climbing the cliff in the open air, high above the jungle. At times the going was easier, with little winding pathways snaking around the tall orange spire; but at other times it was much harder, and they had to use all their strength and skill to make their way up. Mostly the rock was solid, and they could rely on foot holds and hand holds, but every now and then great chunks crumbled and gave way.

Higher and higher they climbed. All of them were tired, but they knew they had to press on if they hoped to make it to the top before the jungle night descended.

Suddenly, Lara slipped. She was pulling herself up over a difficult over-hang, when the whole rock she was leaning on gave way.

She screamed and fell. Jack braced himself, clinging tightly to the rock face. This was why they were tied together; if one fell, the other two might save them - if only they could hold on. But the force of Lara's fall jerked the rope around Jack's waist so suddenly that he was pulled backwards and his hands were ripped from the rock, his feet slipped and he also fell.

This time Claws braced himself. As Jack fell, the rope went taught, pulling hard at where it was tied to the cat.

Now both Lara and Jack were hanging from the rope, and if Claws fell that would be the end of all of them.

The cat frowned, straining with effort; he dug the claws on all six of his legs as hard as he could into the rock, and held fast with all his strength. He had to give Jack and Lara time to get back on the rock face again; until then he had to hold their weight.

Lara and Jack both reached out and grabbed a hand hold. It was hard to find a grip; but first Lara managed to grab hold, and then Jack. They pulled themselves in against the cliff and found footholds to take their weight.

Finally, Claws could relax his grip on the rock. They were safe. All three of the climbers clung onto the cliff, breathing heavily.

Claws pointed up ahead to where there was a ledge. The three of them clambered up and round onto it. At last they could rest. They collapsed, exhausted.

"Well, no one said this would be easy!" said Jack.

"Thanks, Claws," said Lara.

"Yes, thank you," repeated Jack. "You saved our lives."

Claws smiled and nodded. Without their new friend, their lives and their voyage through the galaxy would have ended right there - in a long fall from the cliff.

They sat for a while on the ledge, drinking from their water flasks.

Lara inquisitively followed the ledge around a little and saw that it led to a small cave. Then, as she put her hand on the rock, she found that it stuck there. She looked and found that there was a transparent sticky substance in a long, thin strand stretching across the rock.

"Yuk!" she said, and did her best to wipe her hand to get rid of it.

Meanwhile, Jack leaned his head back and looked up; he could see the silhouettes of the dragons soaring high in the sky around the top of the spire.

His mind wandered onto thoughts of the journey ahead. When they reached the top, somehow they would have to get past the dragons if they wanted to get the jewel from the cave.

Jack was worried. He had no plan for that part of the mission yet. They would have to solve that problem later.

"Come on, we'd better get moving," said Lara.

"Agreed," said Jack.

Claws nodded and they began climbing again, very grateful that they had Claws to lead the way.

They had climbed ten metres or so when a movement caught Jack's eye. Something was moving on the cliff above. It was small and white, and was climbing quickly down the face of the cliff. As it came closer Jack could hear a faint, high pitched cry of alarm coming from the little creature.

"Minnow! Minnow!" it called in little, urgent shrieks.

"Look!" Jack called to the others. "Do you see that?"

Claws and Lara looked up and saw

the little creature hurrying down the cliff towards them. It wasn't much more than a ball of fluff, but it had thin, little arms and legs, which it used to swing itself down the rock.

Then another movement caught Jack's eye. Lara and Claws saw them too. Now they knew what the little animal was running from.

"Spiders!" cried Lara.

Lara didn't like spiders. They had always made her feel creepy; and these spiders were like none she had ever seen before.

They were huge. Each had a black body over a foot long, with a great, bulbous abdomen and sharp, spiky legs. About twenty of them silently and swiftly descended the cliff in pursuit of the fluffy, white creature.

"Minnow! Minnow!" the creature cried again.

It was now quite close to them; and as it half climbed, half tumbled down the cliff; it slipped and fell.

Instinctively Jack reached out and caught it. The little animal was stricken with fear, and it chattered in a high pitched voice:

"Minnow, minnow!"

Then as Jack brought it towards him, the little thing buried itself into his chest, burrowing down into the top of his jacket. Under the white fluff, Jack could just make out little eyes, peeping out, wide with fear.

"Hey, little buddy," said Jack, "don't worry, I won't let them get you!"

Jack had a fondness for little creatures, especially cute, furry ones. At the abbey he often used to feed the white mice which sometimes wandered into the kitchens. He had saved a few from the cook's traps and had secretly cared for them in his room before releasing them somewhere safe. Several he kept on feeding for many weeks. For a moment he wondered what had happened to them and if they were safe.

On the mountains near the abbey he had spent hours watching the little mammals that lived in the nooks and crannies high in the rocky peaks. He knew many life forms, but this one was new to him, its fur was snow white, its arms tucked away into its fur as it hid, so that it just looked like a white ball of fluff, but when it extended its arms, they were pale pink, surprisingly long, and they ended in tiny monkey-like hands which now gripped the edge of Jack's jacket.

A shower of loose rocks disturbed Jack from his thoughts. Looking up, he saw that the spiders were steadily making their way down the cliff after the little creature. They clearly had plans to make him into an easy meal.

Jack held on with one hand and unhooked his crossbow. He fired. With a flash of red, a laser-blast shot out at the nearest spider; its body exploded, and what remained of it dropped off the cliff.

The spiders had seen them now, and undaunted by the blast from Jack's crossbow, they came on even faster. It was clear that the companions were now on the spiders' menu too.

Lara unclipped her laser spear and waited until one came close; then with a swift, fluid move, she ignited the weapon and cut the spider straight down the middle. The two halves fell either side of her and disappeared to the ground far below.

Still clinging to the rock with his feet and one pair of arms, Claws used his extra set of arms to draw two laser pistols from his belt holsters and began blasting the spiders.

Jack managed to take out a few

more with his laser crossbow, but they were coming on too fast.

Suddenly, one of the arachnids leapt in the air. Extending a strand of web from its swollen abdomen, it swung down the cliff and landed on Lara's back, trying to stab her with the jagged barb on the end of its belly. Lara could smell the putrid aroma of rotting flesh emanating from the spider as it scraped at her with its sharp legs.

Jack quickly took aim and fired. It was lucky he was a good shot, or else he might have hit Lara; but his aim was perfect, and the spider was blasted off Lara's back before it could pierce her with its poisoned barb. It fell away with a screech.

The other spiders tried the same trick, leaping in the air, and dropping fast on thick strands of web.

Claws and Jack had to blast them mid-air, otherwise the black arachnids would have landed directly on top of them. The spiders were so numerous that every shot had to count. A miss from their laser weapons would mean the spiders would get to them. Stinking pieces of charred spider showered down on top of the three climbers, as they fought furiously to defend themselves.

Lara held up her spear and fended off the giant beasts; she had to wait until they were close to be able to hit them, and so the wiry legs of each spider almost reached her before she could slice it with the laser tip of her spear.

Clinging to the vertical cliff face and fighting the spiders was exhausting, and as one spider leapt at Jack his foot slipped. His shot missed. The laser blast flew past the spider, as it launched itself in a ferocious attack.

It reached out with its spiked legs, trying to attach itself to Jack; he managed to grasp hold of it with one hand to keep the stinking creature off him. The spike from the spider's abdomen stabbed over and over. Jack managed to twist this way and that to avoid its barbed end which oozed green poison.

"Jack!" cried Lara.

She couldn't get to him. Spiders rained down from above her, and she couldn't leave her own battle for a moment, or a spider would have her too.

Claws tried to blast the spider as it attacked Jack, but Jack was swinging from side to side and was moving too quickly for Claws to get a clear shot; he couldn't fire at the spider for fear of hitting Jack.

Eventually Claws managed to get a good aim and fired; but just at that moment Jack slipped again, and the laser bolt missed and went wide.

Claws was just taking aim again when

a spider leapt through the air and landed right on him too; its poisoned abdomen spike levelling a killer blow right at the cat's head.

Claws let out a shrieking hiss, bracing for certain death; but it never came. Instead the spider froze, then, with a swift, scuttling movement, it rushed off.

The other spiders also suddenly abandoned their attack and silently disappeared down the cliff face.

The companions gasped for breath.

"Are you OK?" called Lara.

"Yes!" Jack called back.

"Claws! Are you OK?" shouted Jack.

Claws gave a 'thumbs up' sign.

Lara clambered up to Jack to make sure that he was alright.

"The last thing we needed up here were giant spiders!" gasped Jack.

Lara's face went pale.

"They weren't giant spiders," she whispered. "That's a giant spider!"

Chapter 11

The Giant Spider

Jack followed Lara's horrified gaze, and his jaw dropped. Silently descending the cliff-face, directly towards them, was an immense spider.

Its body was over three metres long, it had enormous spiked legs and a massive belly; it was black, like the other spiders, but its stomach was stretched and bulbous, and red veins snaked all over it. Even from this distance, the stench from the monstrous beast reached their noses.

Jack raised his crossbow. He fired a blast at the gargantuan arachnid, but the lasers just bounced off the legs. They were coated in some kind of black shell, as strong as metal.

Claws tried to blast it too, this time hitting the body. The spider didn't even flinch, and the blast deflected off the great, armoured hulk of its abdomen. It continued its calm, steady approach, in no rush, and with no fear, simply making its way towards its evening meal – them.

"Quick! Back down to the ledge!" shouted Lara, shaking them out of their petrified horror.

The three companions scrambled down as quickly as they could. They could see dozens of eyes on the spider's beady head staring at them, intent on its victims, measuring the distance for its killer leap.

Below its head flexed great, razor-sharp jaws, and behind it, a huge, jagged spike hung from its grotesque belly; it scraped down the cliff leaving a long gouge in the rock, filled with globules of acidic, green poison that fizzed and bubbled in a long trail.

Jack, Lara and Claws moved swiftly along the ledge, keeping as quiet as possible in the vain hope that silence might delay the inevitable attack.

"In here!" gasped Lara.

She pointed to the little cave she had seen earlier. The entrance was just big enough to allow them to enter. They had no idea what might be lurking inside, but they had no choice - whatever might be in there, it was better than what was stalking them outside!

They scrambled in, pushing forward into the darkness, cramped against each other and the hard, stone walls.

Then two things happened at once - the giant spider outside, working out their plan to escape, leapt down on a thick rope of web, and with a great scraping and tumbling of rocks, it thrust its fangs into the cave entrance, just missing Claws who had been the last to enter.

At the same time they realised they were not alone in the cave.

One of the spiders they had been battling earlier had also decided to take refuge inside, and now, backed into a corner, it attacked.

Lara had been the first in the cave, and the spider lurched towards her, its many eyes shining devilishly in the low light, and its fangs slashing at her face.

Instinctively, she simply punched it. The beast fell backwards, stunned for a moment; it was all the time Lara needed. She whisked out her spear, ignited it, and thrust the laser end straight into the spider's dribbling mouth; she pushed it home right through its body. It collapsed with a crunch and a hiss of charred flesh.

The giant spider outside would not be so easy to deal with. It scraped and clawed at the entrance to the cave with its fangs and legs. Some of the rocks around the entrance of the cave began to collapse. It would not be long before it dug them out.

They were trapped in the darkness, pressed against the stinking corpse of the spider Lara had just killed. They were running out of time.

The only light inside the cave was from the device strapped to Jack's wrist.

"Wait a minute!" he exclaimed. "42! 42! Can you hear me?" Jack shouted at the communicator.

"Aah, hello, sir!" the metallic voice of the big robot began. "I was wondering when you would be in contact. I am pleased to say the repairs on the Silver FOX are complete, ahead of schedule..."

"42! Shut up and listen to me!" interrupted Jack. "How quickly can you get to our location?"

42 looked at the navi-com screen. "I can be there in moments sir, the ship is ready. I can navigate to you immediately. I am on my way," he said calmly and efficiently.

Sensing the panic in Jack's voice, the Centurion didn't wait to ask what was happening, but acted at once. He started up the engines of the Silver FOX, and soon the little ship rose above the jungle canopy and was speeding low over the tree tops towards Spire Mountain.

Inside the cave, Jack, Lara and Claws cowered away from the probing legs and jaws of the immense spider, as it tried to get at them.

"Listen!" said Jack, suddenly.

At first it was very faint, but then soon it was unmistakable - the distant hum of the FOX's engine, getting steadily louder as the little ship drew closer.

"Wow! Yes! I never thought I'd be so glad to hear that ship!" laughed Jack.

Lara laughed too and hugged him, but their moment of relief was short lived.

Their cries had enraged the spider outside; furious at being denied its food for so long, it had renewed its efforts to get at them, and now it began rapidly scratching at the cave entrance with its front four legs. The technique was working - it had nearly reached them.

To make matters worse, just as quickly as the sound of the Silver FOX had reached their ears; it disappeared again.

"Where is he?" exclaimed Jack. "What's he doing? Why doesn't he fly up here and just blast it? 42! 42! Where are you?" he shouted in desperation.

The robot's calm, metallic voice came over the intercom.

"I couldn't hover close to you without the dragons being alerted to our presence. They are very near your position and I could not risk the destruction of the Silver FOX. Stay where you are. I am coming."

"Stay where you are!" snorted Jack, "- great advice!"

The three companions were now squeezed more tightly than they thought possible at the back of the cave, completely piled on top of each other. Jack managed to kick the dead spider out towards the cave entrance to make a little more space. Immediately the jaws of the giant spider outside caught it; and they watched in disgust as it was diced and shredded into tiny pieces before it disappeared into the filthy drooling mouth of the horrific beast. Unless something happened soon, it would be them disappearing down inside its stinking throat.

Then a new sound reached their ears. It was a steady, rhythmic, thumping sound. The giant spider heard it too and looked up, distracted from its attack, wondering for a moment if it could find easier food.

The thumping noise grew closer and louder, now they could hear a clanging noise too; something large and heavy was coming up the cliff.

"42!" guessed Lara.

The spider was now fully alert. No longer thinking that the noise might mean food, but considering it a threat to its territory, it turned and waited, poised to attack.

Jack peered out of the cave. There was 42, climbing swiftly up the cliff. His hands held the rock in a vice-like grip and from his feet six-inch spikes protruded and he kicked them into the rock, with each step creating an instant foothold.

With a hiss, the spider launched itself down the cliff and leapt at 42. Trying to bite his head with its monstrous jaws, it wrapped its legs around the robot's body.

42 did nothing. He turned his head towards the companions, and they heard his usual, deep, calm voice through Jack's inter-com:

"Good bye, Jack," he said simply.

Then, Centurion 42 let go.

He fell and the spider fell with him. Held in the grip of the robot's metal hands, the spider shrieked as it disappeared. 42 said nothing more. He was gone.

Jack stared after him. 42 had saved their lives again. He had said that he needed to earn their trust, and now

he had - but it had cost him his life.
Even though 42 was a kill-bot, the
same sort of machine that had killed
his parents, the same that had
destroyed the abbey - 42 had been
different.

Somehow that had given Jack hope,
and now he could not help but feel
that he would miss the big robot.

But he had no time to think about that
now.

"Let's go!" said Lara and the three
made their way quickly up the cliff.

They scrambled up, climbing ever
higher, until at last they came to a
broad ledge, and there in front of
them was the dragon cave.

Chapter 12

The Green Jewel

Lara, Jack and Claws gazed into the yawning entrance of the cave. Keeping close to the walls, they kept themselves pressed against the rock to avoid detection.

So far the dragons in the sky had not noticed them, and they hoped to sneak in and out of the cave without being seen. It wasn't much of a plan, but it was all they had.

They entered the cave and looked about them. It was huge, filled with strangely sculptured rock formations that looked like bizarre, contorted creatures. The floor and walls were scratched and gouged by the talons of many generations of mighty dragons.

The strangest thing was that the whole cave was bathed in a green glow from a light that seem to emanate from behind a large formation of boulders at the back of the cave. The companions made their way deeper into the damp darkness, the green glow just enough for them to see by.

Suddenly, Jack stopped. The others froze. Jack pointed down to his left. Lara and Claws looked to see what he was pointing at.

At first Lara couldn't make it out. It looked like a long, smooth rock, pointed at one end. Then slowly she realised what it was - the giant claw of an immense dragon. It lay still, asleep, its body blending perfectly with the rock around it. Now they saw that the strange shaped boulders were in fact its huge body.

The three companions stared in horror at the claw, then they looked slowly up and along the dragon's great, scaled, muscular legs, round the broad, ridged back and along its thick neck; eventually they had turned right round and were now looking straight at the dragon's huge head; it was right in front of them. As their eyes adjusted to the dim green light, its features became clear.

How had they missed it? What should they do now? They stood absolutely still.

Fortunately, the dragon was asleep. Its eyes were closed and its breathing was slow and steady. Then it shifted a little, took a long, slow breath, and exhaled with a deep, contented sigh, blasting Jack, Lara and Claws with hot air from its nostrils.

They had to go on, but one false step and the dragon would wake, and it would be the end of them.

They tip-toed slowly forward, creeping towards the glowing light. Jack held the Omicron; the arrows on the device pointed directly at the light source. The green light must be coming from the jewel itself. They were so close! If only they could get the jewel and escape to the Silver FOX without the dragons even knowing they were there.

They crept past the sleeping dragon and on towards the very back of the cave and the light source. The eerie green light shone more brightly than ever around them.

Lara nudged Jack; she showed him her scanner and risked a whisper.

"Look! - Zeta-radiation. No wonder the dragons where acting so aggressively."

Jack nodded. The green jewel's power had reacted with the rocks about it and the resultant chemicals had affected the mighty beasts and made them far more aggressive and dangerous than they would ever usually be.

Then, they saw it. Sitting on a ledge, at the back of the cave, was the green jewel. Glowing fiercely and causing the rocks around it to glow with leaked zeta-radiation.

Perhaps the dragons thought that it was special? Was that why it was in such an important place? For this was no ordinary section of the cave - it was a nursery.

Curled up in little nests of three or four, entwined with each other in blissful infant slumber, were dozens of baby dragons.

The three companions stopped and stared. Facing dragons was bad enough, in fact it was pretty much suicidal; but facing a dragon which thought you were threatening its young was complete madness! One sound from just one infant dragon would wake their immense, sleeping guardian, and the companions would be dragon-meat!

They inched slowly across the dragon nursery. Treading softly and being careful not to make the slightest noise. They made their way towards the green jewel, passing dozens of sleeping beasts.

At last they reached the far wall. Lara and Claws waited anxiously, glancing round at the sleeping reptiles, whilst Jack quietly climbed up to the ledge which held the precious jewel.

He couldn't believe he was so close! Suddenly his foot slipped and a shower of rocks cascaded down onto the cave floor below. Jack froze, looking round with concern that he'd woken the dragon infants.

Lara and Claws crouched down. Several of the infants stirred, disturbed by the noise, but they settled back to sleep.

"Phew!" Jack whispered to himself.

He continued his climb, pulled himself up to the ledge, and there in front of him, shining green, was the first Omicron jewel.

He reached out and took hold of it. It was cool to the touch. The zeta-radiation it emitted was harmless in small doses, but suddenly, Jack felt nervous - what other powers might it hold? Why had someone gone to all these lengths to hide it?

It was too late for questions like that now. It was his, and it would help him destroy Vendax; that was all that mattered. He held it in one hand so that he could still see by its light and carefully climbed down to the others.

They had done it! The jewel was theirs! But they still had to get out of the cave, past the dragons, and down the cliff to the Silver FOX. It wasn't over yet!

With smiles on their faces at their success, the three adventurers turned back towards the entrance of the cave; but as soon as they turned, they stopped, and their jaws dropped.

They were face-to-face with dozens of pairs of open eyes. The dragon infants were no longer asleep.

The creatures had been roused by the noise and the cool breeze of the early evening; it was their usual feeding time.

They were awake and they were hungry!

Chapter 13

The Dragons of Doom

"OK…" gulped Lara.

The dragons looked inquisitively at the three strangers. They were not afraid, not aggressive, but they were curious, and very interested in Lara, Jack and Claws - these unusual beings that had entered their cave.

The baby dragons uttered little, chirping noises in their throats and their gaze never left the companions, but they had not yet worked out that they might be food.

"Come on," said Jack, "slowly!"

So far, the dragon infants had been

quiet. If only the three of them could creep past before they woke the larger dragon, it might just be alright. They might still escape!

Jack, Lara and Claws, picked their way through the dragon bodies, but the young reptiles were becoming more restless, fascinated by the visitors, they pressed in front of one another for a better view. They were becoming bolder, and several of the bigger ones sniffed at the companions, beginning to consider that if they were not dangerous, perhaps they were edible.

The three adventurers moved more quickly, the little dragons followed, and now they were beginning to make a lot of noise, trilling and squawking with interest and excitement.

Now the companions were so close to the huge body of the adult dragon that they couldn't believe it hadn't been woken up by the noise of the dragon babies - if only they could just sneak by.

They rounded a corner, and there was the adult dragon. Unfortunately, it was not asleep. It was fully awake.

Even though its head still rested on the floor of the cave, and it hadn't yet moved, the huge dragon's eyes were open, and it had been quietly watching them.

Now they were captivated by its gaze; slowly it began to lift its great, horned head. Frozen with fear, they watched as its neck stretched, lifting its head higher and higher, until finally it stared down at them from the ceiling of the cave.

Then they heard a movement beyond the dragon. Slowly the huge reptile moved its body to the side, and now they had a clear view of the entrance to the cave. It was not alone.

The whole cave was now filled with

adult dragons; their silhouettes dark in front of the red, sunset sky. Their eyes glinted green in the light of the stone that Jack still held.

At their head stood a huge creature; he was clearly the leader. He was scarred and old, and as the other dragons made a move forward, he snarled at them with a deep warning tone, making sure that his flock were exactly where he wanted them. If there was a meal to be had, he would decide who fed first. Any route of escape was completely cut off. Jack, Lara and Claws were utterly trapped. It was certainly the end.

The dragon infants behind them, although small in comparison to their larger parents, were still the height of a human, and quite capable of killing. Now they pressed forward, clucking and chirping with excitement, their hunger and their numbers making them brave; they began snapping at Jack, Lara and Claws, who jumped to avoid their razor-sharp teeth.

The huge dragon leader lowered his head and issued a low, fiercesome growl, stopping the companions in their tracks. He could easily kill them with the tiniest movement of his head or talons; yet all he did was prevent them escaping.

"Oh dear," said Lara, "I think they are teaching their infants how to hunt."

"Teaching them to hunt? What do you mean?" asked Jack. "Oh," he gulped with realisation. "You mean the babies are going to hunt us? What a way to go, breakfast for baby dragons!"

Lara nodded. Somehow the thought of being pecked to pieces by fledgling dragons was even more horrific than being devoured by one of the larger beasts; although neither prospect was good, at least one would be quick. Only a miracle could save them now.

Just then the little, fluffy creature in Jack's shirt stirred. Jack had almost forgotten about it. Earlier, he had been worried that the little thing had been completely crushed, as they tried to hide from the giant spider.

"Minnow, minnow," it chirped.

Holding the top of Jack's jacket with its tiny, pink hands, it pulled the top of its small, white body out and shook its head to clear the fur from its eyes.

As it looked up and saw the dragons, it uttered a small sound:

"Uh-Oh!"

The reaction of the dragons was surprising. So far they had been utterly cool, calm, and menacing. Now they looked agitated at the sight of the little creature. The lead dragon pulled his head right back; all the adult dragons shifted on their feet and visibly retreated as they saw the fluffy animal. Several dragons on the ledge even turned and took to the wing. Only the infant dragons seemed undaunted and continued their investigative snapping at the companions. One of the larger fledglings boldly stepped forward and positioned itself ready for the kill.

The white, fluffy creature looked about him from the safety of Jack's jacket. He seemed to be appraising the situation.

"Ah ha!" he said. "Minnow!"

Then he brushed his hands together in a no-nonsense, business-like way and sprang from Jack's coat.

At this movement, many of the dragons moaned and moved backwards away from the furry creature, which now stood on its two, fully extended, little, pink legs, with its hands on its hips.

It lifted its head and began to sing a long high-pitched note:

"Minoooooooooowww!" it sang.

The note went on and on, and gradually the pitch got higher and higher.

The dragons turned and fled, bumping into one another, scrambling towards the ledge to get away.

The infant dragons looked at first bemused; then as the pitch of the note got higher and higher, they began to shake their heads in discomfort, and then in pain.

Some retreated to the back of the cave shaking their heads, their eyes closed tight, screeching in agony at the sound. Others followed their parents and flew off the ledge; although unsteady and inexperienced fliers, they preferred to risk the air than suffer the noise that the small, fluffy creature was making.

With its little lips pursed, eyes closed in concentration, arms now extended fully to either side, with its tiny fingers wiggling with enjoyment; the little, fluffy creature continued making the noise until all the dragons had fled away.

Then the little creature stopped making the sound. He turned to Jack and said:

"Minnow?" raising his arms as if to say: 'Is that OK?'

Jack, Lara and Claws laughed.

"Minnow?" replied Jack. "Well, come on, little 'Minnow', come with us! Let's get out of here, before the dragons change their minds and come back!"

The journey down the cliff was much quicker and easier than the way up; and very soon in the last rays of the sun, Jack, Lara and Claws stood at the base of the cliff again, Minnow sitting on Jack's shoulder.

"Well that was certainly a day I'll never forget," said Lara, gazing back up at the cliff. Claws nodded.

Then they turned toward the Silver FOX. It was right at the base of the cliff; it was fixed and ready for departure.

"Good old 42," whispered Lara.

Next to the Silver FOX lay the crumpled body of the giant spider. They looked at it warily, and suddenly, to their horror, it began to move!

They quickly drew their weapons. Minnow shrieked, and jumped to hide in Jack's jacket - but it was not what they thought.

Clambering across the body of the spider, causing it to wobble, was 42!

The kill-bot looked battered and scratched, in one hand he held his own arm which had broken off in his fall, but he was alive!

"42!" exclaimed Jack.

"You're OK!" cried Lara.

"The body of the arachnid broke my fall," said 42, in his calm, deep, voice. "I have a few minor injuries, but other than that, I am fully functional."

Claws, however, was not so excited. Even though Lara and Jack had told him that 42 was harmless, at the sudden appearance of a kill-bot, he quickly took aim with his four laser pistols.

"It's OK! Claws!" said Jack, "he's a friend! You can trust him! We can all trust him. He's more than earned it."

Nodding with understanding, Claws lowered his weapons and returned them to their holsters on his belt.

Jack approached 42. "Hey 42, it's good to see you in one piece, well almost one piece. Don't worry; I'll be able to fix that arm for you," said Jack.

"Thank you, sir, I trust you to do a good

job," replied the robot.

"And I trust you," said Jack. "Thanks, we would not have made it without you."

"You are welcome, sir," said 42.

"We would not have made it without any of you," Jack continued, looking at Minnow and Claws.

"42, may I introduce the two newest members of our team: This is Claws, and this is Minnow. Claws, Minnow - this is 42; and we owe all of you our lives."

Claws bowed low to 42, and Minnow chirped happily:

"Minnow! Minnow!"

Lara smiled.

"Now let's get out of here before it gets completely dark," said Jack. "This planet is truly beautiful, but I have had quite enough of its wildlife for one day!"

"Lara, thanks, you are one tough girl!" added Jack and slapped Lara on the back as he walked towards the Silver FOX.

For a moment Lara looked sad. A 'tough girl', was that all he thought of her?

Jack walked towards the Silver FOX, Minnow perched on his shoulder; behind came Lara, quiet and thoughtful, the red light of sunset shimmering over her long, dark hair; beside her the gallant Claws, his fur fluttering in the twilight breeze, and finally, 42, giant, steady and strong.

The five of them walked up the service-ramp and entered the hatch-way of the Silver FOX. The door closed behind them.

They were quite a team; and they would need to be. This was only the beginning. They still had five jewels to find and a whole galaxy to cross in order to find them. Then they would have to face Vendax himself. It was going to be quite a voyage.

Chapter 14

Vendax

Far away in the depths of space, on board a giant terror-naught destroyer a tall, white figure stands rigid and still, gazing at the spectacle of a dazzling nebula spread out in the stars before him.

On his console a green light begins to rapidly pulse. The figure slowly turns his head and looks at it.

An officer in an immaculate uniform approaches the console nervously.

"My Lord Vendax, is that the signal you have been waiting for?"

"Yes, Commander. Ready your men. Prepare to attack."

The deep, powerful voice of the colossal, white robot - Vendax, commander of all the kill-bot armies, ruler of the galaxy, is ruthless, cold, and utterly evil.

"Yes! Lord Vendax," replies the commander and he hastily moves away.

Vendax is alone again; he looks at the pulsing, green light on his console. His black eyes stare from his white mask-like face, and his lips remain frozen in a permanent, enigmatic smile.

Then from deep within his chest there comes a sound. Vendax is laughing.

"So!" he says in his booming voice. "You have found the first jewel for the 'Omicron'. Good! - Let the chase begin!"

To be continued.....

Galaxy Voyage Part 2:

The Sandvipers of Zaak

Jack, Lara, 42, Claws and Minnow continue their heroic voyage across the galaxy in this next exciting installment of the Galaxy Voyage trilogy.

The crew of the Silver FOX are whisked onwards on their dangerous journey - first to the ice planet of Sowan, where in the frozen wastelands, they face a host of monstrous snow-beasts; then to the desert planet of Zaak, where with new found friends, they battle gigantic scorpions and killer snakes in search of the next crystal jewels for the Omicron.

With Vendax and his robot armies in relentless pursuit, this action-packed sequel propels the companions from one danger to another in their continuing quest across the stars.

Galaxy Voyage Part 3:

The Disc on Shard

In the dramatic conclusion to the Galaxy Voyage trilogy, Jack and Lara face Lord Vendax himself in a final, lethal showdown.

With help from friends across the galaxy, the companions must hunt for the last of the Omicron crystals in the wild city of Electra, beneath the waves of the water-world of Lanza, and on the volcanic planet Shard.

With danger at every turn, facing terrifying, alien creatures, and with Vendax unleashing all his forces to stop them, the crew of the Silver FOX will need all their skills and all the luck in the stars, if they are to finally complete their quest to find all the Omicron jewels, defeat Vendax, and restore justice to the galaxy.

About the author

L.D.P. Stead

Laurence Stead is a primary school teacher, and father of two, who lives in Brighton, England.

His interests include: movies, playing and recording music, photography and video, collecting retro toys, walking in the countryside, art and design, history and science.

Galaxy Voyage is his debut as a children's fiction writer and is a celebration of his life-long enjoyment of science fiction, fantasy and adventure stories.

www.galaxy-voyage.co.uk

8636: 1R00078

Made in the USA
Columbia, SC
13 January 2018